THE GUIDE

TRENT BOWER

LAMPLIGHT LITERATURE LLC

To my amazing and beautiful mother and sister. May the light and warmth of my soul always reach you. Know that you are never truly in darkness, and the love I have for you is infinite and unyielding.

<u>Author's Note</u>

I'll begin by stating that I am by no means an expert in the field of psychology or mental health. In fact, this story, although rooted in real experiences, is nothing more than a fictitious sliver of much larger, much deeper issues. While this book is ultimately for entertainment, my intention is to ensure that each character and experience has been properly, and respectfully, represented. I think it is also important to recognize that mental illness manifests differently for everyone and may require different approaches from what the narrator in this story does. With that in mind, I continue to believe there is great value in finding a genuine support system and vocalizing problems when they arise, at least as I have come to know based on my own life experiences. Now, without further delay, I present to you: *The Guide.*

"You are braver than you believe, stronger than you seem, and smarter than you think."

~Pooh's Grand Adventure: The Search for Christopher Robin

<u>1</u>

It was fleeting. Quick, even. I expected a massive surge of pain when my head hit the river bottom, but it was anticlimactic. One moment I was at the top of the bridge peering down, and the next minute I was gone. Honestly, I wasn't certain what would happen next, and I wondered as the pitch-black void shrouded me if I would simply lose my consciousness and fade away. I wasn't an avid believer of anything, really, so I had nothing to cling to in my final moments. I guess, for me, the decision to commit suicide was the only thought that mattered in the moment. Days of shouting at one another; our house had felt like a warzone. My mother and father were so busy attacking one another that no matter where I retreated with my brother in tow, it still wasn't enough to escape the yelling and the crying. What's worse was when the attacks were directed at me. Being told to "stop crying" or "get over it" coursed right through me like a bullet striking through paper. But couldn't anyone see that I was doing my best? I had been fighting nonstop to hold my optimism, to be the pillar of support that my family needed me to be. By the end, I could barely force a fake smile. With a million problems in the world, I felt like I had no right to add another one with my own pain, so I suffered in silence. I thought maybe I could handle it all. Stay strong like Atlas. But I'm sure even that weight became too heavy for him to bear. It certainly did for me.

Genuinely, I was just so tired, and it felt like no one would care if I simply slipped away. Always the background character or the canvas beneath the artwork — never to shine or be admired. It's tragic, but it was only in my final moments that I began to wonder what would become of my little brother and my mother. Right about now, they were probably worried sick. Naturally, my father would be cursing my name in anger for creating this commotion. What of my best friend? He was probably wondering why I didn't text back or answer any of his missed calls. What would he do when the news hit him? I was sure he'd be fine. Really, they all would be. Maybe I should've written a better note, though. At the time, I poured what was left of my heart and soul into it. Now that I looked back, that was all I left them to remember me by. My final days were a series of arguments at the dining table – spiteful words without love and full of ill intention. I should have said I loved them, at least once. A final hug to remind them that even though I was leaving this world, it had nothing to do with them.

I suppose that was all irrelevant now. A decision was made, and the price was paid, but was it the right decision? Unfortunately, there was no taking it back.

Damn, I thought.

Why now was I starting to regret it? Why now did I realize that I was loved, at least by one or two others? Now that it was too late, I saw that I wasn't simply the canvas beneath the art; to some, I was the art. Confusing at times, I'm sure, and yet they still saw the beauty. If only I had realized before I leapt.

Interesting, isn't it, lost one?

"Who's there? What's interesting? Isn't this meant to be the end? Aren't I meant to silently exit into the abyss?" It was a bit unsettling to have my final moments of self-reflection interrupted by a voice outside my own. "'Lost one,'" I echoed. I wasn't sure how I felt about that nickname.

Questions. There are always questions. For now, consider me a guide or a mentor. Someda—

"Oh! So, you're like Virgil, right? Or Charon? The reaper, maybe? I've read a book or two. I'm starting to get the picture here."

No. Just a guide. Someday, I hope you come to consider me a close friend, but for now I'm here simply to guide you. Before you oh-so-enthusiastically interrupt with more questions, let me explain. It's interesting that in your final moments you elect to remember what you couldn't even see when you were alive…

Oh. So, I was dead after all. I shouldn't have been surprised or upset, but I was. I guess I just wished it was a horrible dream, and maybe I could wake up. Maybe I could embrace my mother once more. Maybe laugh with my little brother again.

…I see that you've tuned out. That's fair. It's only natural to take this as a shock. Yes, well, it remains interesting that only now are you beginning to realize the consequences of your actions outside of yourself.

"Wait. Wait. Please. Is this normal when people pass to the afterlife? Is there some way to go back? Can I undo what I've done? It was a mistake, I swear. A hastily made decision after a long period of pain and sadness. I thought it was my only option."

Tragic as it may be, what you've elected to do cannot be undone. Your decision is final. Any temporary problems you have faced have now been met with a final, absolute answer. There are no do-overs, and there's no way to bring you back.

"This is really it, isn't it? So, now am I headed to the afterlife? What's waiting for me? Am I bound for hell because I wasn't devout? Is there a heaven that will take mercy on me for the pain I've endured?"

The afterlife is different for everyone. Some seek what they describe to be a heaven and a hell. Others seek Valhalla. Some aim for Elysium. The truth is it's catered to whatever the person believes in. I'm not here to pass judgement or provide a specific path for every soul that comes through. My purpose here is to dictate what souls have done well or badly morally. Did you live a life that directly hurt others? Did you live a life that could have helped others? That's what matters most. Were you a good person? Is the world better, even at a microscopic level, because of you? From there, I just determine if you get a "good" afterlife or a "bad" one.

"I can't say that I've done my best. I don't think I helped anyone, directly or indirectly. I honestly felt like I didn't really matter to anyone, at least while I was alive…"

Lost as you may be, you were kind to many when you were alive. You may not have seen the light that guided others, and you may not have felt the warmth you gave to others, but you were both a light and a source of warmth to those in need. When you checked up on classmates who would otherwise ignore you, when you sat around with your little brother to watch him play games despite how tired you were, when you comforted your mother as she cried despite how sad you were, you were warmth. You were light. Perhaps what's most tragic is that you ended your story before you could finish writing it; before you could extend that warmth and that light to others.

"I wish I had known."

There was a pause as both me and this entity sat in silence for a moment. It was all so much to process, and I felt my heart crack with each word I repeated back to myself. Each moment of realization had pierced right through me, and I couldn't take it. I was overcome with emotion, and for a moment, everything became just too heavy to handle, causing silent tears to rain from my eyes.

"So, what now? Is it time for me to move on?"

Well, that's for you to decide. You have taken your life, and, with it, your story. However, I see the light that emanates from your soul. You can choose to move forward into your eternal slumber, or you can stay behind and become an apprentice to me. Before you decide, let me share with you two things. First, I don't just help the departed. I have spent — and will continue to spend — countless years trying to help those that are still alive. Like a guardian angel or simply just a voice from beyond. I act in a way that consoles their hurting and helps talk them off the ledge for whatever hasty decision may come to pass.

"Why didn't you help me, then? Where was your voice when I needed it? Where were you when I cried myself to sleep? When I suffered in silence? When I felt like I was losing myself, why couldn't I hear you tell me that I was going to be okay?" I couldn't help but interrupt. I was angry and confused. It wasn't that the idea of helping others wasn't enticing; I was envious because I had needed that same help too. Maybe if someone, or something, had reached out when I was alive, I would have still been there. Maybe all I needed was to know that someone cared — that I wasn't so alone.

The second thing you should know is that this is not something I ask just anyone. For most, including the tired and lost souls that elect to end their stories early, it truly is the end. You are an exception. Do not begin to think that everyone has this choice when they pass — just you. Why? Because your soul has such powerful light emitting from within that your voice can reach the living. I watched over you, and I know what your potential is. However, the choice remains yours. You can choose to be the voice that others need to hear. You can lift the tortured and breaking souls and prevent the same kind of tragedy that you met. Conversely, you can rest and let go of that which tethers you to your former life. I will warn you, choosing to carry your light will not be easy. You will not save everyone. You will feel the pain and sorrow of helplessness. Simply put, this is a path filled with thorns.

"Huh" was all that I could muster. I could cut all ties and finally rest, and that would mean letting go of everything good and bad alike. When I committed suicide, I felt like the only thing I wanted was to let go, but now I wasn't so sure. This felt like a second chance. It wouldn't be the same as getting to live once more; I couldn't be there to watch my brother play his games or be the shoulder for my mother to cry on. I couldn't even help my classmates or my friends in the same ways, but this choice would allow me to help ease their minds and bring them peace. I had the chance to help people continue their stories, something I ended prematurely.

"I'm in. Please let me guide others and ease the burden on their souls."

And just like that, the pitch-black shroud was lifted. I saw that this entity was simply a person like me. The two of us were surrounded by silhouettes of various shapes, sizes, and auras. These must have been the souls of the departed, and yet they all felt and looked so different. No two were exactly alike. This person before me — my guide, so to speak — was equally hard to identify. Despite being a complete stranger, there was still a familiar presence about him. He didn't loom over me, and he didn't carry a heavy aura around him. In fact, it was quite the opposite. He had this blinding yet soft, warm light enveloping his body. It was comfortable to be in his presence, and I could understand why so many souls would willingly listen to him, whether they'd departed or remained ongoing.

Wonderful. He smiled. *It's time to begin our journey, lost one.*

<u>2</u>

"So, where do we start? I think I know what you do, but I don't know how you do it." I had to question it. There was no logic in any of this, and it all felt like magic to me. The problem, of course, was that I was a skeptic.

I take it you wouldn't be satisfied if I simply told you it was magic, would you? What if I had no answer at all?

Wow. A mind reader, I thought.

I can tell just by your perturbed look and blank stare that those answers wouldn't satisfy you. It almost feels as though I'm wasting your time, but that can't be true, can it? After all, we pretty much have forever at this point. All the time in the world, as it were.

"Fair enough." I couldn't help but admit that zinger was well-played. For someone who seemed to have been around since the dawn of time, he sure was witty. I couldn't help but like that personality. If I had to spend eternity with someone, I was glad it wasn't some brooding and pensive individual. I was certain that my eternal workload would feel far more daunting if that were the case.

Look, the fact of the matter is that we exist outside of the realm of the living, but we're not quite in the realm of the dead either. Think of a balloon. There's air on the exterior and there's air on the interior, and with time, that interior air will escape out. That's simple logic, right? Well, the living realm is like the air inside the balloon. People — their souls, their consciousness, their thoughts — are held within this "balloon," and those thoughts, those feelings, and those souls all contain energy which passes to the grand "exterior" where we reside. Generally, this is a one-way passage, but we exist, not necessarily as gate-keepers, but more so as observers. Is this starting to make sense?

"Actually, yes!" Still, there were holes in my understanding and other questions that I felt would simply cause us to spiral down a rabbit hole. I imagined I could spend an eternity trying to understand these realms, but this was good enough for me. "Okay, so with all this information coming at us, how do we navigate to the voices we need to help? I feel like it's an endless stream of data, and I feel like we'd get lost along the way, wouldn't we?"

Brilliant questions. Here's the overarching answer: You listen. He paused to gauge my reaction. *Ah, there's that dissatisfied look again. It's like this: You need to focus on what you're trying to find. It's an act of tuning out information that we don't need, in hopes of finding the information that we do. It's not easy at first, but with practice you'll be able to pick up on that sensation almost immediately. Have you noticed why you don't really hear anything or see any particular energy passing through? Because you're not really focusing on it. Why don't we give it an attempt? You can start by clearing your mind and focusing on listening to the world around you.*

"Okay, but I have one more question before we begin. It's off-topic, but I've been wondering since you appeared, and I know I won't be able to focus until I get an answer. May I ask?"

Well, you already asked a question when you asked me if you could ask a question in the first place, but sure. What is it?

"You know what I meant." I was unamused. "So, here's my actual question: How did you even get here?"

Excuse me? Why is that something that's on your mind?

"Well, you come off as this ancient being, right? I feel like I could have read history books about you. Or maybe mythological books. Have you always been here? For all I know, you could've been around since the birth of humanity. But if that were the case, how do you know so much about modern things like balloons — how does that work?"

Your crude humor aside, the question regarding my origin is irrelevant and almost certainly a waste of time. Moreover, we clearly have work to do on your listening skills. Didn't you hear me when I said we were observers? We pay attention to the times as they change. People evolve, just as our thoughts and customs do. Societal norms are all temporary constructs — entirely dependent upon the society you're in. We merely listen and watch the evolutions take place.

"Well, now look who has the dissatisfied look on their face. If I remember correctly, though, we 'pretty much have forever at this point,' right? 'All the time in the world, as it were?'" I couldn't help but grin as I said it. After all, I had an eternity to spend with this guy as my mentor and business partner, so I might as well crack some jokes every once in a while. At the very least, it looked like he smiled too.

Touché. Now talk less and listen more.

And that's exactly what I did. I stopped talking, sat down, and started listening. It was pure silence. There was literally nothing to latch onto. Not even a whisper. Calling it frustrating would be putting it mildly. Again, I felt like I was surrounded in complete darkness. It was all so empty here, but that couldn't be true, so why was it that I was unable to hear anything?

Finally, I muttered to myself, "It must be my thoughts. I need to clear my mind completely, just like with meditation. Maybe if I can just allow everything to come into my mind, I can start narrowing down what I want to pick up on. Perfect. I'll give that a go. Just breathe. Focus. Listen…"

Suddenly, a blip. Just for a single moment I heard something. I didn't know who it was from, and I couldn't hold on to that voice for too long, but I was able to catch just a single sentence: "I feel so alone."

"I did it!" I opened my eyes and saw the blurred image of my mentor looking back at me. No emotion one way or another, but he did speak.

Well done. You've managed to pick up on a voice, or so it would seem. It also looks as though you've managed to catch the emotion attached to those words. Otherwise, why would you be crying?

"What are you… Oh." Before I knew it, I felt the teardrops rain down my face and shatter on the ground. But why? Was I just relieved that I managed to do something? It couldn't be as simple as that. I was excited, but there wasn't much to go off. It was merely a starting point, and I happened to pick it up quickly. I hadn't realized we could also feel the emotions attached to the words we heard. It felt unfair. How were we supposed to act as these impartial observers if we felt every single emotion that was attached to the words and the thoughts that we heard?

Empathy. It's a funny thing, isn't it? We have to be able to pull someone out of their rut and help them, but can you really help someone if you don't actually know how they feel? Are you really listening to someone if you don't feel the emotional weight of their words? I do recall mentioning this wouldn't be easy, and I think now you're beginning to understand a bit better as to why that is. Can you really help anyone if you don't understand where they're coming from? Yes — this is a lesson on listening both to someone's words and also to their pain. Don't be discouraged; you're doing a fine job. Let's begin again, shall we?

"Okay." I started again. Clearing my mind was simple; there were no thoughts left in it. I was ready to take on anything that came my way, but again, I was met with silence. There were a few murmurs here and there, but nothing distinct. After an extended time sitting in silence, I began to feel foolish.

"You know what? I've done this once already. Why don't we just jump to the part where I start helping someone in need? You could stick around and give me some pointers or even get me started, but I think I can handle it, especially if I'm able to able to visualize the scene with someone. I can't imagine it'll be too difficult to tune in when I have more sensory stimulation to help me out."

Hmm. Curious. I'll entertain this experiment of yours, but what happens if you fail to listen? Can you still help someone? Remember, actions have consequences, and that includes our own.

"Yeah, yeah, yeah. I got this. Trust me, okay?" It was a bit of a bluff. I thought I could help someone, but I honestly couldn't say that for certain. I was feigning confidence, but I didn't think it could be that hard.

Okay. If you believe you are prepared, then let's go.

In less than a moment's notice, our whole environment changed. What was once a waystation filled with wandering souls became a dingy living room. There was trash everywhere, ranging from pizza boxes with molding leftovers to empty plastic bottles of whiskey, everything scattered all over the place. There was barely any furniture and some of the lights either flickered or were burnt out. The entire place was in a state of disarray, and at the center of it all lay a woman slumped over and defeated, looking at the remnants of a shattered jar. Her clothes were covered in filth and grime, desperately needing a wash. It didn't take much detective work to realize exactly what we were dealing with.

"So why this person? This woman doesn't need the help that we can provide. She needs AA or rehab.

Something more on the physical and social side, not the mental one."

You should try listening. You may be surprised. That's why we're here in the first place, isn't it? Because you were so confident her words would reach you.

"I did mention that. I guess you're right." Tuning in proved to be more difficult than I originally expected, and I kept asking myself why it mattered. One look and I could see that the problem was her poor choices, not something deeper.

She's been suffering, that much is clear. But tell me what you're thinking about her situation. How can we make a difference here? Talk to me.

I took a deep sigh before speaking. "Look, she just needs to get it together. Drinking yourself into oblivion doesn't help anyone, least of all you. The empty bottles of cheap booze and the disgusting state of her house only go to show that her priorities don't chalk up too much. Best thing to do here is to step it up, get clean, and watch the problems dissipate. It's that simple."

Careful now. Regardless of choices made in the past, someone can still have a bright future if given the chance. If she's an addict, the help we can provide is empowerment to seek help. We can help her realize that she is still worthy enough to get the help she needs — to step back onto the correct path. You need to remember that your words hold power. Without direction, those same words that are meant to help can strike right through someone. Harsh words don't often build; they break instead.

"Why is that a concern? It's not like she can hear us. And honestly, sometimes harsh words can make a difference for the better. It was a choice to drink heavily, and the same is true for not drinking. It's a choice not to. Let me help console people who really need it. At least someone more deserv—"

In that moment, the woman burst into tears, and I caught bits and pieces of what she said. She mumbled on about her own guilt. She cried about how she could have done things differently and made better choices. Something about "stepping up" and doing what was right, and yet she cried on about being unworthy and undeserving of help. It was eerily similar to what I had just said, and that was when it clicked. Despite my inability to hear, I was still able to speak, and she could've heard me, maybe as a manifestation of her own conscience.

You're beginning to understand, aren't you? It's easier to speak than it is to listen. That is just as true in life as it is in death. If you had taken this even slightly more seriously, you could have caught the bigger picture. This isn't some game you get to play half-heartedly until you're bored. As I said, your words have power, just as they did when you were alive. The choice to spew hateful thoughts and dismissive behavior without any attempt to comprehend the situation just goes to prove that you're nowhere near ready to begin. What you failed to hear was this woman's story. She is working both mornings and evenings every night between two different jobs just to afford the medical bills that her son needs for a heart transplant. Not only is the stress overtaking her with bill after bill slowly burying her alive like quicksand, but she's trying to balance it all without any support. She has no family to turn to and no partner to help carry the weight, whether it be financial or emotional. What she does have is a housemate who is rarely around but coerces her into drinking, hence the liquor bottles. She blames herself because she got pregnant so young and chose to stop her education just to ensure her baby could be healthy; being a mother is a full-time job, whether you choose to think so or not. From there, she continued to blame herself for her son's poor health since she couldn't give him the proper nutrition while pregnant.

"I didn't know. It all seemed so obvious at first."

That's the issue. You spoke without even trying to empathize. Don't you see that this woman feels as though she's undeserving of help because of what you said? You put this notion in her mind that she made poor decisions and doesn't deserve the same chances as someone else. You don't get to take that back and pretend like it didn't matter. One glance at the state of her home, her attire, and her mannerisms and you wrote her off as nothing more than an alcoholic without a care in the world. If that were truly the case, we wouldn't have come here in the first place. Think about it: The mountains of trash and empty bottles are because she's so busy working. She can't focus on picking up any messes. You really think if given the chance to see her son or clean up her house, she'd choose her fleeting time to clean? Of course not. Let's keep going. Can you tell me why she has this defeated look?

"I, uh, I..." There was no time to prepare my thoughts. I was blindsided by one thing after another.

Examine closely and you'll see that shattered jar she's gripping onto. That had probably been the savings she had built up. What if it was meant to be a gift for her son, or what if it was for something more crucial? Regardless, now it's gone. Why act defeated if you willingly spent that money? Huh? It's because she didn't; it was taken. It's moments like these that can make or break someone. They could crumble from the strain and fall to bad influences or merely give up, accepting defeat. Some certainly find comfort at the end of a bottle; that's entirely possible to see in this case, given that alcohol is something she has constant exposure to. You see, putting negative energy back into someone's mind can spiral them down a path that could otherwise be avoided. What path do you think you sent her down by casting her aside that first instance in which you saw but didn't listen?

"Okay!" I snapped. "Okay. I understand. I realize I was overzealous and went about this whole thing half-assed. I acknowledge that I need to do better and look beyond what my eyes can see. Please, just tell me there's something we can do for her. Can we do something to alter her course?"

We don't get to decide the fate of another. We merely attempt to usher in proactive thoughts that can empower someone to make a difference in their own life. The truth is I'm not some omnipotent being that can change things with the wave of my finger. Sometimes our voices don't reach when we really need them to. Sometimes someone's consumed with negative thoughts and can't find a way past them or we simply can't reach them in time. Everything's a possibility.

"Why are you telling me this? I already blame myself enough for my judgmental and surface-level evaluation. Knowing I might not get the chance to push her on the right course only works to defeat me. So, why are you giving me such a harsh lesson?" I may have become just an aura, but the pain I felt was real. The dread and guilt of knowing I hadn't taken things seriously enough began to overtake me

This truth is inevitable sometimes. You are destined to fail at one point or another. I, too, have failed many times in my attempts to help. I watched you on that bridge, and I swear that even the heavens could hear me screaming out to you, begging for you to hear me. Unfortunately, you won't save everyone that you meet. It's fair to say that most people we see in our lifetimes have a whole world of struggle and strife that we have no idea about. They may appear one way or another, but we have no clue what they're going through or what they're feeling. That's where our predicament gives you and me the advantage. You see, we're able to go past that surface level. We're able to feel the pain that most don't ever have the chance to see when they're living. So no, you won't be able to save everyone, but you can try.

"Okay. I will. I need your help to do so, but I want to. I see that this isn't something to take lightly, and I understand why we're here now. I want to make a difference, even if it's minor, and I want it to start here, with this woman."

Come along, Icarus. Now that you've been burnt by your sun, you should have a better appreciation for it. For now, just pay attention. I will do my best to help this time, and you will listen. To me, and to her.

3

It was beautiful to hear the guide speak to the woman. He was empathetic and understanding, but most of all, he removed her sense of guilt. The agony and anger — it all dissipated as they spoke. I think it may have been the first time in her entire life that she felt heard. When he finished speaking with her, there was a sense of peace to her. He made it so that she could make conclusions and find answers to her own problems. I realized that his job wasn't to give an answer, but rather just to remove the pain and the haste of any decision.

In a flash, we were gone and back in our own realm, observing the world with a bird's-eye view. After a long pause, I gathered as much strength as I could muster and said, "So how do you know? Like, how do you know it worked out? Did she find a way to make it work? Do we get to learn more about what's next?"

I'll put it simply: You don't. There's no reward for helping someone with their anguish. You just do it because you should. We do the things we do because we can. Nothing more, nothing less. If you're looking for some form of closure, I would offer this: You succeed each time you don't see someone you're trying to save end up in this realm right after.

"So, what do you do… when you fail? How do you recover from that sorrow?" Maybe I shouldn't have asked that, but I couldn't help but wonder what that was like for him to deal with. I quickly regretted asking, realizing that my question could only bring pain and just served to satisfy my curiosity.

Despite what I expected to be a pained reaction, he merely smiled. Although it was clear there was hurt behind that mask, he responded. *Well, we're already dead, so it doesn't really matter how we feel. You can spend eternity dwelling on those feelings and failures, or you can move forward and let go. Easier said than done, of course, but what you learn today you can put into practice tomorrow.*

"Does it ever get tiring? Having all that wisdom?" As soon as I asked it, I realized just how unnecessary my quip was, but with how heavy the work was, I thought it might be fun to lighten the mood. If he had been all alone before this, it couldn't have been easy to cope with each experience.

Much to my surprise, he played along. *Exhausting, really. They say beauty is pain; well, wisdom is suffering. All jokes aside, it's time to jump back in. Are you ready to try again? This time without the training wheels?*

"Well, I'm feeling pretty exhausted after a long day's work. It might be nice to rest."

Funny, but let's go. You can rest when you're dead… Well, I guess not. He chuckled.

Cheeky. I'd give him that. "Wisdom is suffering. Yeah, I'm really learning that quick."

Great. This next poor soul is but a young child, from what I can tell. This boy has self-esteem issues which probably stem from some body dysmorphia he has. I've been watching over him for a little while, and I can tell that it first came about when the ones that he called friends made fun of his weight and tarnished his self-worth. He has a family who loves him, but unfortunately it seems like they're just too busy, so I think he feels unseen and unheard. He seems to feel alone and desperately just wants to be cared for.

Unfortunately, this feeling was all too real to me. It didn't take any special skills to understand exactly where this poor kid was coming from. That tragic feeling was made even clearer when we arrived to a dark room littered with stuffed animals and a boy curled up in a ball, silently crying. It was crushing to think that despite all his suffering, he was still trying to keep from bothering his family. It was as if he felt like his very existence was problematic, so to receive love, he took on all of his own problems and smiled through his suffering. It appeared that it was only when he found himself alone in his room, left with only his stuffed animals and his thoughts, that he shattered — like stained glass against jagged stone. Every night he wept without noise until he fell asleep. His sadness only manifested as resentment. His mind clearly stated, "I can't be loved. It's because I'm weak, and I'm disgusting. I'm nothing. My friends point and laugh at me like I'm just there for entertainment, and I'm constantly reminded by those around me just how overweight I am." Through the choked words and silent tears, I heard his muffled voice say, "But I'm trying." He continued, "Why do I have to suffer this way? I just want friends who don't hurt me. If I have to become an unbreakable force to stop feeling this way, I'll do it. I will gladly do whatever it takes; I just don't want to feel so alone anymore."

My first thought echoed that of the guide's. I remembered feeling this way at one point in time. I knew the road he was starting to walk down. I also knew just how important it was to reach him, and I kept thinking: It has to reach him. I spoke softly but clearly. "I hear you. I know you're struggling, but you don't want to become a source of fear in an effort to protect your heart. I know it sounds tempting to become this pillar of strength by closing off your problems, but this will make you crumble away. You don't want this — just trust me."

"I just want to be loved. I don't want the weight of my body to be seen before the weight of my heart," he said. "But maybe I don't deserve it. Even my own dad doesn't want to be around me. He left so long ago, and I almost never see him now. My mom is busy trying to make things work, and I see that, but I just want to be heard. I want to be told that it's going to be okay. I don't want to have to keep pretending so that the others don't worry. I'm just a kid, and I'm at the point of eating meal replacements instead of real food. I wear baggy clothes in the scorching heat because they aren't form-fitting and can hide my stomach. It's miserable, and if becoming a scary, hateful version of myself is the faster solution, I want it. I'm tired of feeling this way."

Hearing him talk about how he was just trying to survive was heart wrenching. As my heart cracked for this boy, I answered, "I understand, and I know you're in pain. Believe me, I can see that you've been strong for your busy family. I can see that you've tried to be strong for their sake too, haven't you? Though your dad isn't around that much, I'm sure you wish he would show up, even if it is just so that you can get one more minute with him. No one should ever have to feel as though they need to be on a diet in order to obtain love and affection from others. You're pushing hard, and you are truly a sweet boy with so much love to give. Putting on an angry and isolating façade isn't who you are — it only serves to push away those around you. Hold on to the ones that do love you, and work hard for them. The rest don't matter. With the way the world is, don't succumb to what's easy. Give love to a hateful world and change it for the better. It won't always be easy, and you may fail at times, but keep holding on to the morals that make you such a kind soul. Don't deprive yourself of what makes you so beautiful, and always let the light of your love shine onto others so that they too may be able to grow for the better."

"But I'm so scared. What if I never find the people who love me as I am? Then what do I do? I'll be alone."

I could tell that the boy was still struggling to come to terms with everything. In hopes of calming his heart, I offered him one last piece of advice. "Be true to yourself. There will come a day when the right people love you and want you in their lives. Don't be afraid to love, and you'll never be alone again."

And with that, the boy walked to the light switch and turned on the lights. Once more, we were back in our own realm.

<u>4</u>

Well done with that situation. You certainly had an impact, and it seems like that came from deep within. Was that something you've personally experienced?

"In all honesty, yes, that came from the heart. I've been there. I was there my whole life, and people were always cruel. Part of the reason I was even on that bridge in the first place was because of what hateful people said. Of course, not everyone says things with the intention of those words reaching someone, but sometimes they do. The thing is sometimes that cruelty doesn't just bring about pain and sadness, but also anger. I imagine that boy's desire to be feared stemmed from the same pain. We just took different routes." I paused in reflection. It's not something I was ever open about, but I guessed things would've been drastically different if I had been heard and not just seen. "So, you've experienced tons of lives and emotions, but most of them were strangers, right? Have you ever had to help someone you've met before? That must be especially hard, right?"

A very peculiar question, but I certainly have. It's especially difficult to endure that experience. Even our closest friends and family only know what we tell them. Sure, we can assume how someone is feeling, but there's really no way of knowing unless they tell you, and people only tell you what they're ready for you to hear. The greatest displeasure of our work is when we finally learn about the pain and suffering our loved ones have quietly endured without us knowing. Why do you ask? Are you worried for someone's sake?

"I am. A bit. It's about my best friend. He's an incredible person, but he doesn't have many friends. I guess I'm worried that despite how wonderful he is, people in our school and even at his home will continue to mistreat him. The reason he and I became so close was because the both of us were often outcasted by others, and I know he'll continue being ridiculed and ostracized. It's frustrating because they'll completely miss out on the chance to meet someone spectacular because they're too enamored with fitting in. Sometimes I just wish he didn't have to think about any of this at all." I had to pause because I could sense the frustration starting to boil over inside of me.

Ah. Well, isn't it a bit egotistical to think your friend can't stand on his own two feet? It seems wrong to assume that he's in constant need of protection. Maybe having you as a friend was enough for him to live life just fine. It doesn't take an army of supporters to feel heard. Sometimes it just takes one good listener. Moreover, have you ever considered that he hadn't even thought about being outcasted, especially with you by his side?

"Well, no. I actually didn't."

Almost immediately, I realized how foolish I had sounded. I didn't even need to look up to know there was an annoyed expression on the guide's face.

Do you know how many wonderful souls I've met — both in their reality and ours? Too many. Do you know what they all had in common? They were all missed by the ones that loved them. Not a single one of them had first considered what they lost, but rather who. Your friend is no different. I can guarantee he's the exact same as the rest – missing you dearly and not even remotely concerned with the people who pay him no mind anyways. Your largest concern should be realizing that there will come a day when your friend will face isolation once more, but this time he'll need to face it without a friend by his side. To that end, wouldn't it be a better question to ask how your friend might be feeling at the loss of someone he cared for? What guilt do you imagine he feels at the thought of not being able to save you? You were able to keep him out of isolation, but how do you think he feels knowing he couldn't do the same for you?

"Whoa. Whoa. Okay, but that's not his fault in the slightest. I had so many other external factors going on that he wouldn't have even known about. There's no reason for him to feel any form of guilt. It's not his fault." I was beginning to feel guilt of my own.

The realization of who I left behind was starting to creep up again.

Didn't I say this already? People only tell you—

"What they're ready for you to hear, I know. You do know that your infinite archive of wisdom can be quite burdensome, right?"

Well, you have an eternity to get over it.

"This is a very hostile work environment, you know? Also, I'd like to talk about the hours we're expected to work. Don't even get me started on that. It's egregious what the hours are! The pay is a bare minimum. And my boss—" I stopped when I heard him chuckle, which took me by surprise. I had started to believe that there were only two emotions with this guy: neutral and less neutral.

Alright, comedian. We're not done working. Let's check on your friend. It's a bit unorthodox, but it's not unreasonable for you to help someone you know, and I have a feeling this won't be the only time. Plus, it also gives you the chance to see him again, which is a nice perk.

I looked at him in surprise. "Wait. I'm sorry. I just thought you didn't approve of us visiting him."

No, that's not so at all. I believe that your heart has always been in the right place, I just wanted to give you a different perspective about why we should pay him a visit. Consider it guidance from someone with a lot of experience.

Our surroundings took on the shape of a familiar place: a bedroom with walls littered with posters and floors with dirty laundry. It was a typical teenager's room, but this one belonged to my best friend. There were memories here — attachments and connections. I remembered all the times we laughed and cried together. We stayed up all night and slept all day in this small, safe space. I'd never taken a single measurement of this room, yet I remembered every inch. Every corner contained a crystal-clear memory. At the center of it all sat a boy gripping onto a photograph, afraid that a loose grip would make the photograph drift away from his memories. All that I could see in this room, once filled with joy, was sorrow. Tears flooded down his face like a river rushing down a cliff. I could feel it all; there was anger and there was guilt, but most of all there was loss.

When you die, you don't get to decide how people feel. You can't choose which people remember your light. Some people, like this young man, felt the warmth that emanated from your soul, and when you snuffed out your own flame, you left those around you shrouded in a cold emptiness. You may have chosen to jump, but the ones that loved you were forced to fall, too.

"I realize that there are ramifications to my actions, and I acknowledge that you've been teaching me this. In all honesty, though, none of that is particularly important to me at this very moment. What matters right here, in this moment, is helping to pick him back up. I was given the chance to guide people, so what would be the point if I can't do everything in my power to guide the people I care about?"

Suddenly, I heard a familiar voice call out, "Why? Why did you have to go? Why didn't you let me in? Was it pride or something else holding you back from talking to me? You weren't just my best friend, you were my only friend, and now that you're gone, I'm all alone again — just like before. Did I do something wrong? How long were you suffering without me even knowing?" His voice broke, and no words could escape any longer.

"Hey. Hey. It's not like that at all. It's…" My voice wasn't reaching. He couldn't hear me, but I needed him to, just like with the boy from earlier. "I need you to hear me. I need you to know it was never anything you did wrong. I may have left, but I didn't leave you." There was nothing in response.

Through tears and whimpering, all I could hear was, "I'm sorry. If I had done more—"

It was heartbreaking to watch him suffer, and it was frustrating to feel so helpless at the same time. I wasn't sure what to say to pierce the veil between our realms, but despite that, I stood beside him while he wept. I wasn't sure if it would work, but I placed my hand on his shoulder, hoping that he could feel my presence. Then, I spoke up. "Danny, whether you're able to hear me or not, you have to know that it was never your fault. You did more than enough as a friend, and even though I couldn't keep running alongside you in the marathon of our lives, you were able to prolong my race for just a little longer. You did enough, man. I promise."

Tears subsided into a deep slumber. Maybe it was the weeping that left him too exhausted to stay awake, or maybe my words were finally able to reach him. Even as I wondered which was the case, I knew that I couldn't ever be certain. After all, we don't really know what someone is thinking or feeling unless they tell us.

<u>**5**</u>

Training commenced and I continued to listen, but it was tough not to think about all the people we met, and I struggled with wondering whether we were really doing any good. The guide's words kept repeating in my head: *We can hope, and we can continue trying, but here success is only measured by the absence of someone's essence in our realm.*

"How do you do it? How do you continue moving forward with such confidence when there's no guarantee of success?" I finally asked.

I put one foot in front of the other and continue walking my path. I have doubts and struggles all the same. I question myself and my actions each time I try to help someone. There is a reward to this when you succeed. You won't necessarily experience it right away, but eventually you will.

"Well, what is it? What's the grand prize waiting for us?" My interest had been piqued at this point. I needed some way of knowing I could have that gratification — to know that success was tangible. I needed proof of my work.

It's more so that we're waiting for it, not that it's waiting for us. See, take your friend, for instance. You will know that you've successfully guided him if you see his aura here in maybe sixty or seventy years. You understand what I'm getting at here, right? You'll finally find him on this side of reality, but it will be because his story has been fully written. At that time, you can finally ask him what his life was like. He can fill you in on all the things you missed, and you can have that closure. For others, it would just depend on when they pass away, and that could be sooner or later. I can't really give specifics beyond that.

"So, have you been able to catch up with people from your past, known and unknown?"

Of course. I'm a guide to the afterlife too, you know, not just a guide for the living. I get to see all the faces of people as they move on, which means being able to catch up with them, too. I always make the time to hear their stories, and it makes it all worth it — even on the hard days.

"Interesting. I underst—"

We need to leave right now. All conversation can wait until later. It's an emergency.

As he finished saying this, I was thrust into our new reality, but this felt different. Unlike before, he was frantic, and we were searching. It wasn't some controlled environment where time was practically irrelevant like it usually was. I was getting nervous.

"What's going on?" I whispered.

We're looking for someone in dire need of help. She's in a bad place, and it's a critical moment. I don't know what's going on, and I don't know if we're already too late, but right now what matters is looking for this person, because if we can't find her, we'll be seeing her in our realm very, very shortly. Understand what I'm saying here?

"All too well, unfortunately." Just as I finished speaking, we were shrouded in a downpour. Everything was dark. The streetlights flickered frantically, almost as if they too understood the urgency of our arrival. Normally, the two of us would work together like a mentor and mentee, but this time he hurried off, echoing, *Separately… cover… grou*— and he vanished. It was unsettling to be in this scenery, and it felt so familiar and so cold.

"Well, only way to get something done is to get it started," I said under my breath, and off I went. "Let's see. If this were me, I'd probably seek out somewhere quiet and away from the world." I remembered that when I was alive, the best way to escape the weight of the world's problems was simply to find a place away from the world — somewhere I could just exist without struggle. It wasn't much to go on, but it was a start. "Hmm, maybe I could walk away from the houses and toward something more isolated. It's possible there's a scenic area or outlook just beyond this area. That'd be somewhere where someone could be an observer but not have to participate."

As I walked away from the house lights, it continued to get colder and darker. It was as if the very feeling of life was fleeing from this place. Darkness began to swallow the whole region, and all that interrupted the endless void were the intermittent pools of light from the streetlamps above.

I kept getting an eerie feeling as I walked. I started walking faster — the feeling remained. Faster — the eeriness continued. I began running, but eeriness blossomed into panic. Where was she? Had I gone the correct way? What if I took too long trying to figure things out?

I needed to calm my nerves, so I whispered to myself, "Stop. Get out of your own head. You can't afford to feel hopeless, especially not until you know for certain what's happening." Despite the pep talk, I was still sprinting, and I wasn't just frantic, I was afraid. I didn't want to lose a chance to help. I couldn't afford to.

Then, I came to a clearing. Only a few hundred feet ahead of me was a bridge. It was freezing outside, and my body was convulsing. The rain felt like a barrage of ice, and even the light from the lamps wasn't enough as they dimmed away. But there she was, standing just under the pale, dim light in the middle of the sleek bridge. I watched as she stood there, just looking down at the darkness below, gaining a false sense of confidence in an irreparable mistake.

Then it hit me. She and I were the exact same.

<u>6</u>

"Hey. Hey you. Just a moment. Please. Don't do anything too hasty, okay?" I spoke before I even had time to think.

"But I'm tired." She answered as if she had heard the same lines countless times prior. How hard did she have it? How long had she struggled just to find a place where the world simply happened around her, and she could become a passenger, merely drifting?

"Look, you don't know me, and I can't begin to imagine what pain you've been through, but I know this feeling. I've lived this feeling. Believe it or not, we have that sense of suffering in common. Right now, I would guess that you feel as though you don't matter. Maybe your value amounts to nothing. Maybe you've been strong for so long, but even the most durable pillars can crumble when they have too much pressure. This exact moment, this a breaking point. Sound about right so far?"

"Sounds about right. Can't say you're helping, though."

"Well, here's the lesson I missed, the one you need to hear, especially now. You matter. You have value. This feeling is a low point, but it's momentary. You're about to make a permanent solution to a temporary problem."

"But what if you're wrong? How do you even know?"

"I don't. But I do know working up from your worst day is something you can do to continue living. You have the chance to get the help you need and learn your value. You're not at fault for feeling this way. You just need a little bit of help, and that's okay. Everyone needs help from time to time."

"I just… I just feel like I don't deserve it." Even in the rain, her tears stood out. It was heartbreaking. Hadn't someone tried to reach out to her? Couldn't they see her pain?

"Listen to me. No matter who you are, no matter what you've done in life, everyone deserves to get help."

She began inching closer to the edge. "I just don't want to burden anyone."

"Look, look, just hold off on making any decisions while we have this conversation, okay?" The stress made me feel like I was walking a tightrope on the tallest building in the world without a safety net, and the rope was beginning to fray. "Listen. You're not a burden for asking for help. When you help others, it brings you joy right? Well, think about how others might feel when they can ease your pain and quiet your thoughts? There are people out there who will listen. There are people who want to listen. You aren't alone in this world."

…

"I promise. Please don't do this. You have your whole life to live. Please don't make the same mistake I did."

"Maybe… maybe you're right. I just don't know." She took a deep breath. It looked like her tears had subsided.

My god. This is working. I can't stop now, I thought.

She was at the bridge's edge now. She continued, "But what if this is the easier option?"

"You have your whole life to find the happiness and joy that you've been seeking. If you make this choice right now, you may stop any difficulties from coming your way, but you won't get the chance to experience some of life's greatest joys. There is beauty in this world. I may have missed my chance, but you still have one."

"You could be right, but you don't know when this crushing feeling will subside. It could be as soon as tomorrow, or I may only have fleeting moments of joy. Unfortunately, I think I'm at my limit." She took a step up onto the railing.

"Wait. WAIT!" Things were going so well. I just wanted my words to reach her.

"Thank you." Another step. Standing on the edge of an abyss. At a crossroads.

"Please. Don't do this." Tears rushing down my face. Never had I felt so desperate. "You don't need to do this. Okay?"

She closed her eyes and spoke silently just one last time. "I'm sorry."

"Ple—please! STOP. NO. N—"

<u>7</u>

"I'm back? No. No no no. We're not done. We have to go back right now." I was gasping for air, overtaken by and overwhelmed with tears.

You found her?

"We need to go back now. I can… I can catch you up on this later, but right now we need to leave."

That's not really how this—

Just then, the answer revealed itself. The answer why we couldn't go back, why we were pulled away from reality, stood before us. There she was, or rather her aura, waiting to cross over.

"She didn't make it." I said to myself before collapsing. My legs could no longer hold anything, and they buckled. I was too weak to stand. I obsessed over what transpired, asking myself, "Didn't my words reach her? What did I do wrong? What did I say that couldn't reach her heart?" This was all wrong.

"Where were you?" I practically screamed. "Couldn't you have done something? You know this better than I do. You should've been the one to speak to her. Maybe she'd still be alive."

I understand that you're hurting. I really do. I know it's not fair, and I know that failing when the stakes are high hurts even more. You feel guilty. Heartbroken. Like the best thing to do is curl up and hide away from reality, right?

"All too right." If I had known this would happen, would I have gone the other direction? Would I have chosen to rest instead? I couldn't say for certain. The guilt I felt was unbearable. I didn't know where to pick myself up from or how to keep moving forward. I wanted to believe this was just an obstacle in my path, but maybe the wall was just too tall for me to climb this time. "I get that you've done this awhile, but I can't really imagine you know how I feel. Do you know what it was like to stand there in the pouring rain and watch someone die before they even stepped off the edge? Do you know the pain I felt watching my words drown out as she moved closer and closer to the edge? The regret I have for not saying enough? What if I said something else, or what if I was there for her in a different way? I watched her mouth the words 'I'm sorry' before she faded into history. There's no way you could feel this weight, is there? I failed. I failed her."

I do know your pain because I failed you. You may not remember this, but I mentioned I was there with you when you were peering over the edge. Desperately, I pleaded for you to hear me, for my words to reach you. All I wanted was to tell you that happiness is achievable. Every moment got darker and darker. Each minute felt like an hour to me. Not only that, but I was there for every moment you felt this way, not just your final one. I failed repeatedly. I thought that I could reach you while you were at the precipice, but unfortunately you never answered back. I watched you struggle and fight for as long as you could, and I've never forgotten that. Just once I wanted you to hear that you weren't alone. Unfortunately, you can't save everyone, no matter how much you try, and I'm entirely aware of this. More often than not, it takes more than kind words to fix things.

"So where do I go from here?"

Forward. You won't save everyone, but you can try to help anyone. Your voice has the power to create just as much as it can destroy. That's as true now as it was when you were alive. Now, go speak with this woman. You may not have been able to save her, but you're in the fortunate position of putting her to rest. Finish what you've started, then we'll begin again.

And so I did. I walked over to the woman who had just found herself in my reality. "Hey, it's you. That person from the bridge," she said as soon as she felt my presence.

"Hey there. Couldn't stay away, huh? I get it. Around this area I'm known as the life of the party." I immediately started asking myself why I was making jokes right now.

"Are you making jokes right now?"

"Oh, yeah. I'm very uncomfortable. This is really not my forte, and I lean on dark humor as a way to make this easier."

She chuckled. "Well, I can't say that I mind. Aren't you worried about getting into trouble with your, uh, boss?"

"Oh, no. Not even a little bit. They can't fire me. Get this, we don't even have an HR department here! Don't even get me started on the pay."

Again another chuckle, and then she became somber. "I'm really sorry about the bridge. I don't want you to think I just didn't listen or that I'm ungrateful. I just..." She trailed off until she stood in silence, looking ashamed.

"There's nothing to apologize for. I'm in this place for having done the same thing. If anything, I get it. I know where your head was, but I'm still glad that you took the time to listen. We were able to talk at least. You didn't have to feel so alone at the end of your life."

"Thank you. Do you mind if I just stay here for a little while to talk with you? I'm not quite ready for whatever happens next."

"Take as long as you need. I will happily stay here with you until you're ready."

Time here was immeasurable and irrelevant, but it felt as though we were able to continue speaking for hours and hours. There was so much she needed to say and to ask. It was clear that there were words that needed to be said and tears that still needed to be shed before she could finally be free. I learned about her trauma and her suffering, but I also got the opportunity to hear about some of her greatest moments. More than anything, we were able to cry and smile together, however fleeting it may have been. We laughed, and I slowly eased her into moving on to what lay beyond. Our conversation began to wind down until it came to a close. Before passing on, she spoke one last time.

"Don't blame yourself. I know you tried, and I don't blame you. I believe you can help others, so please don't give up. And thank you. In my final moments, you gave me some clarity. For the first time in a very long time, I didn't feel so alone. I'm sure if I had a living person say what you said, especially earlier on, the darkness surrounding me might have lifted, even if it was just for a moment, just long enough to find a better solution."

Then she was gone. Her story was over before she had the time to finish it. I was sure to some she was just a statistic. To some, she was just a name without a voice, lost in an endless sea of numbers. She would be forgotten to many but always remembered by the ones that loved her. And to me, she was the reason to keep going.

"Rest now," I whispered then turned back toward the guide, ready to start anew.

<u>8</u>

You did well. Are you ready to keep going?

"More motivated than ever before. Who can we help next?"

The next person we can help is your mother. It appears she's still struggling with your passing. This might be hard on you because she's family and we're rolling right in from an especially difficult moment. I can handle this, if you want me to.

"No. No. I think this is something I have to do." I was steadfast in my resolve. Truthfully, I wasn't always good to her — not as good as I could have been. This wasn't so much a chance to apologize for giving her so much grief, but rather more of an opportunity to say goodbye — properly this time. It was an opportunity that most didn't get.

We found ourselves in a familiar setting once more. A house, not a home — a shroud for four people that had been reduced to three. It felt so cold and lifeless, even my mentor looked like he was shivering. And at the center of this shell, there she was. A single starlight in a dead sky isn't much, but she was enough to shed light. It must have been around dinner time for the family because we watched her preparing food for everyone, staying busy and overdoing it at every turn.

Despite everything that happened, she seemed to be handling herself just fine. She was doing everything she'd been doing while I was still in that house. The only difference was that I wasn't there to help out this time. She was on her own, but she still stood as tall as she did back then. It was only when she moved from her little workstation to the refrigerator that I realized she was struggling. There, taking up a nice portion of her food prep station, was a photo of me, smiling.

Look at that. It seems that in your world — one completely devoid of love — someone held you so close that they couldn't help but keep you beside them every day. It's almost funny to see this photo; you seem to be happy. I wonder what it was that you were thinking about on that day. What made you smile in a way that could fool even me?

"It was a normal day just like any other. There was no special event or occasion. In fact, I distinctly remember that the entire sky was painted gray. Not a single ray of sunlight could penetrate that veil. That smile…" I paused. "That smile was authentic, though. My mother was behind the camera, and before she took the photo she looked right at me and simply said—"

"You are my sunshine," my mother said to the photo. "And now that I can no longer see you grow up, my eyes rain every day. God, I miss you, more than anything in the world. I remember the day I gave you life, and I…" A break. "Well, I just wish I could've kept giving you life. I'd give up everything I have in this world for one more day with you. I just want one more day to see you smile like you did in this photo, my little sunshine." Then she turned around, almost as if she knew I was there, to face me. She had tear-streaked cheeks and puffy eyes. I could tell she had cried even as recently as that morning, and I could guess that she would cry again later that evening.

"Yeah. That's exactly what she said to me, except n… now those same words j… ju…" I couldn't even finish my sentence without weeping. "Now those words just bring me pain. Seeing her like this just hurts my soul."

The guide came over to stand beside me. He embraced me before speaking. *I think your words are better spent with her. It's time to speak up, lost one.*

9

I didn't know where to start. What words could be said to begin to rectify what I had done? Were there any words in the first place?

Finally, I mustered the strength to say, "Hi Mom. It's me. I'm right here in front of you. I'm right here. Please, in some way, please see me. Your little sunshine is right here, okay? It's just that I'm the one watching over you now."

She sobbed and nodded. "I see you, my love." She took a breath, wiped away her tears, and continued, "A bit embarrassing, really. It seems you've come home to catch me as a mess."

"Hey Mom?"

"Yes, sweetheart?"

"I'm sorry. I am so sorry that I left you behind to a colder world. I never meant to hurt you, it's just that, well, it's just that I wanted to stop hurting. I never wanted to cause you this much pain, and I wish that I could have been stronger, like you are."

"My sweet, sweet little baby. You have it all backwards. You were never weak, and it should be me apologizing. I was so caught up in trying to care for your basic needs that I never stopped to check on you and make sure that you weren't burdened by anything. Had I known you were suffering, maybe I could have done something. Maybe I could have helped you receive medication or therapy that might have helped you. Parents are supposed to see everything about their children, even the hidden things. Moreover, a child is supposed to outlive their parents! I blame myself for not seeing the pain you were in, and I'm sorry that I couldn't give you what you needed."

"No. No. Please never blame yourself. You have always been a beacon of hope. My life may have been short, but the person I became was because of you. I saw your love and compassion. Your kindness and your strength. But how did you get to be so strong? For me, it was like stepping into quicksand but only sinking deeper, never able to get out. Doesn't every step you take feel as though you sink further and further into the ground, overburdened by the pressure to live and meet the expectations of everyone around you? How do you move forward when you keep getting pushed back?"

"Well, my love, believe it or not, women can be very strong creatures, especially when they're mothers. We don't get sick days or time off. Tired or hungry, we still need to make sure our little ones get food and sleep. We put everything we are into our children, so no day can go to waste, can it? You see, it's not as though I'm always strong and resilient. Oh no, not even close. It's just that on my weakest days, I still get to see my children, and it's those smiles and that laughter that make me stronger. We keep moving forward to make sure that the suffering we may encounter doesn't reach our loved ones. We do what we do so that the ones we love can continue smiling, unburdened by the weight of the world."

She continued toward the photo, picked it up, and, as she came back to face me, said, "Let me tell you a story about this photograph and why it means so much to me. You see, this day was especially difficult for me. I was struggling with work, had fears that I would lose my job, and was worried I wouldn't be able to support you and your brother. Your father was especially cruel, and a very close friend of mine had just passed away. She too had taken herself before her time. The world felt especially painful that day. It wasn't like sinking in quicksand, but rather like I was in the middle of the ocean during a hurricane. Drowning and being swallowed up. And do you remember what it was that you did?"

"I," I paused for thought. "I honestly can't remember."

"It was a long time ago, so I understand why you might have forgotten. But you took me by the hand, looked me in the eyes, and asked, 'Can we go outside and see the statue in the park?'"

"Oh. Interesting. I'm honestly shocked that I asked that since I never cared for being in that park, nor did I care for that, or any, statue."

"Exactly, but you knew that I loved that park, that I loved that statue. You see, whether you meant to or not, you were trying to comfort me. You could see that I had been beaten down, and your first instinct was to give me comfort. The same things that I was concerned about giving you, you were trying to give in return because—"

"Because I wanted to see you smile."

"You took on my burdens without even realizing it, and you made me strong again. The warmth of your love and compassion felt like the warmth of the sun's rays. Because of you, I was no longer drowning, and I escaped the hurricane of my thoughts. It was only when you smiled that I remembered the importance of protecting you from that same struggle." As she looked down at the photo, she whispered to herself,

"And that moment of joy is immortalized in this single picture, where we were both free of pain."

"I never realized that this moment meant so much to you. But now that I'm gone, does this mean you're going to struggle in the same way you did back then?"

"My dearest, your soul was always more kind than you knew, but your worries are over now. It's time to rest, my child. Please find peace in your slumber. Thank you for giving me this moment, even if it's nothing more than a daydream."

There was a long pause but before leaving I asked, "Hey Mom?"

"Yes, love? What is it? I'm right here listening."

"I love you. Thank you for being there."

"Thank you for being my little baby and for always watching out for me. We miss you, every single day. And I love you. More than you will ever know." My last image of her was watching her smile at me as tears ran down her face. I just hoped that she saw the same from me.

And then I was back in my new realm. My mother went from being a few feet in the distance to being an entire world away. With the change went all the energy I had. It was a bittersweet moment, finally saying goodbye. While it was beautiful for both of us to smile again without burden or care, it was difficult because it was fleeting. We couldn't stay locked in that single moment, but that was okay because it helped me realize that life's impermanence brings value to the love we have for others.

"We didn't really need to check on her, did we? She didn't seem as though she needed anything, and I didn't get the impression that she was about to make a brash decision. Was that for me?"

Well, who's to say? Maybe it was for you, maybe it was for her.

I gave an unconvinced glance to suggest that he wasn't fooling anyone. "Well thank you, for giving me a chance to say goodbye."

This situation bestowed to you certainly can also mean doing things that would otherwise be impossible, like saying goodbye. You may not realize this, but that single conversation, that one isolated moment of closure where she was able to see her lost child one more time, probably saved her life. You were able to visit a struggling person and make them strong once more. Love is a powerful thing.

"Wait, I thought we only find out about the result of our actions by the presence, or lack of it, here in this realm, right? Do we really know that she'll be okay?"

I have not only lived through countless lives, but I have lost countless ones too. Sometimes, it's not the things we say, but the things we don't say that bring people here before their time. Things such as "Goodbye" and "I love you."

"Hey, uh, um…" I trailed off, realizing I'd never learned his name.

Irshad.

"Oh." I paused, shocked that I had never asked prior. It made me wonder what else I didn't know about him. "I never knew learning your name would give me so much peace."

There was a long moment of rest. No words exchanged and no gestures given to suggest anything. Through the constant chaos that had become my reality, this was a moment of repose. Just one moment to stop completely and catch my breath before I finally whispered, "Irshad?"

Yes?

"I'm sorry for the pain you've felt, and I'm sorry that you couldn't save everyone, but I'm here now. You're not alone anymore, and you no longer have to suffer in solitude."

Thank you, for the kindness you've given. Your mother was right; your soul is one of kindness. May I ask you something personal? I overheard your conversation, and it would seem as though I can't quite wrap my head around this, so I've been meaning to ask: Why did she call you her 'little sunshine' anyway? I'd love to know how that came about, beyond what she mentioned.

"It was just from a lullaby that she used to sing to me when I was a baby. The only reason I remember is because she kept doing it throughout my childhood. I can't remember how it goes, but I do remember the sense of peace her song would give me."

There's nothing more beautiful than the unconditional love we share for others.

"And there is nothing more precious than the time we get to share that love."

10

It wasn't too long after the conversation with my mother that Irshad and I became closer. What had originally felt like an eternal punishment began to feel far more bearable with him around. When I had first signed on, I wasn't really sure what to expect, and I certainly hadn't expected to become close friends with him. As it turned out, fate had other plans.

"So, I'm starting to get a better picture of the torture that Sisyphus felt," I said as we continued peering through the veil, looking into the world of the living.

Hah. A laugh echoed out. *He always complained about that rock. I personally would've complained about the hill, but he was quite the character.*

"I'm sorry. Hold on just a moment. Are you making a joke, or are you actually an ancient relic?"

No comment. Besides, you should never ask someone their age!

I snorted, fondly thinking about what a character this guy was. I guess his humor was starting to rub off on me. "Wait, wait. You're avoiding the question. Am I to believe that you actually knew someone that went down in mythology? Just based on the story, it really sounds like you're more likely to be Sisyphus, doesn't it? I wouldn't be surprised. This job certainly feels like a large boulder without an actual end."

His response was a silent shrug which neither confirmed nor denied anything I had asked. It was entirely open-ended, and I was starting to feel like that was intentional.

"But seriously, you could really be Sisyphus. I mean, there's no reason you couldn't alter your name with the unlimited lifetimes you've experienced. All I'm saying is I have my suspicions."

Well, I will let you endlessly wonder about that. I would love to say that I hope this keeps you up at night, but you're not allowed to sleep, so there is that. Anyways, while you ponder one of the ten great questions of the Land of the Lost, let's also look into the work we have to take care of.

"Land of the Lost…?" I trailed off and began to murmur to myself. "Is that what this place is called? On one hand, it is nice to know what my new home is called, but it just leads to more questions. For instance, what are the other nine questions around here?"

Even though I should have been used to the experience at this point, I still got a tightness in my chest whenever we got the call to action. Each time we started to look into who we could help next, I was reminded of the woman I couldn't save. She may have passed on to the other side, but she lived on in my memories, and while I knew that I was taking strides to do better for the next person, I was always reminded of our exchange. There's no concern like the one you feel when someone's life is on the line, and I could tell that I was grappling with how to handle that. It was difficult to guess how I'd deal with another emergency like hers. As I waited for Irshad, I kept wondering if I had grown enough in my abilities, or if I would see the same result and suffer the same anguish as before.

Ah. Okay. Someone needs our help. It's tough to get a read on him though, which makes me think this person is repressing his pain.

"What can we do in these situations? I don't know that I've experienced something of this nature yet."

Well, that's tough to say for certain. I think even for me this is a difficult task, and unfortunately, I can't say that I have an algorithm for us to follow here. It's not easy to be empathic with someone who doesn't show their feelings. First things first, let's see if we can even pierce the veil and speak with him.

The scene we entered was dark and dreary. It felt so far from the light that even I felt cold. The whole place was devoid of color and warmth. In fact, there was no feeling in this space at all. Alone at the edge of a mattress sat a middle-aged man. He was lumped over, almost like a produce bag in a supermarket. At his feet were bottles of alcohol in various states of progress — some completely tapped dry, others in the midst of spilling out onto the carpet. For a time, all we could do was sit there next to him. Neither of us really knew what to say or what to do. The man was quiet and pensive, and while I couldn't begin to imagine where his thoughts were taking him, I could tell that he was fighting a hidden battle within his own mind.

Suddenly he spoke and both Irshad and I jolted up-right. "They say they're my friends, my family, but they don't know anything about me. Isn't it obvious that I'm struggling? I'm under so much pressure that I feel as though I'll burst at any moment. I'm stressed beyond reason, to a point that I can't sleep correctly, and I keep lashing out at those closest to me. I wasn't even that angry with them. I'm just annoyed with myself. I keep telling myself: A man shouldn't show his weaknesses; steel yourself and stop feeling; crying is weak and pointless. I don't have time to stop in my tracks and fall apart. Maybe I can just keep pushing it down. Fake it 'til I make it, right? I don't know, maybe the best thing to do is keep pushing them away. If I keep everyone at arm's length, I know I won't get hurt. It'll be easier not to feel anything that way."

It was then that I realized what he needed to hear. "Maybe you're going about this the complete wrong way."

"Who the hell was that? I just heard you, whoever you are. Where are you hiding?" The man jumped up, not expecting to hear an interloper. In fact, the sudden transformation from lumpy produce to an upright man was enough to startle Irshad.

"Just relax." I spoke slowly and softly. "To you, I'm just a friend watching out for you from above."

"A friend, huh? That's rich. I think I've had one too many this evening." He began to shrug it off and returned to his slumped-over state. "Well, let me tell you something, friend, I'm good. I don't need your help dictating my own life, and, quite frankly, I don't want it."

Slightly agitated, I stated, "Listen. I get it—"

"Oh, do you? What exactly do you get here? I don't need help. I'm doing just fi—fine," he slurred, his drunken state becoming more apparent with each word.

"Fine. Maybe you are doing just fine by yourself, but if that were the case, I don't think you'd be here in this bleak state, would you?"

"H—hey." He belched. "Speak for yourself, okay? This is how I like things, goddammit. I like my solitude, and all those people, those friends, who don't think something's wrong can just piss off. I'm good."

Frustrated, I barked back, "I can see that you're good at talking, but now it's time to listen."

His retort was just belligerent mimicry.

With my blood boiling, I took a deep breath and then said, "You know what? The reason you're alone is that you push everyone away. You pretend that you're fine and that nothing bothers you, but even the best actors can't pretend for as long as you have. It may have started as small disappointments at first — you know, things that you tried to let go of or brush off. When you finally decided to speak up for yourself, I'm sure you heard 'get over it' or 'men don't cry' time and time again. You've experienced so much sorrow, holding back each time out of fear that you'd be ridiculed or rejected by those around you. The pain you've kept inside created small dents in the armor encompassing your heart all this time, and now they've become cracks wide enough for all to see. You're not fooling other people into thinking you're okay; you're just fooling yourself into believing that nothing's wrong."

There wasn't any backtalk this time. No yelling or dismissal. He looked up, almost as though he could see me standing in front of him. "Yes. You're right. I've had to play impenetrable for so long that now I feel as though nothing should faze me. I'm protected this way. I'm safe from getting hurt like I have in the past."

"Somewhere along the way, I think you may have forgotten that this was all an act. It's true that maybe nothing can get to you if you never let it in, but that's true for love and compassion too. Let me ask you something: How do you begin to repair the damage encasing your heart if you never let any of it out?"

"But what if I let it out and the people around me reject me? Then I'm left alone with nothing."

"Aren't you already alone in this state? None of the people you care about know the burden you're carrying. How could they? You aren't being honest with them. You're taking on the burdens and pains all by yourself and pushing those that love you away. You're the creator of your own suffering." I paused for a moment to let it sink in.

I continued, "Showing your emotions isn't showing weakness. You were given these emotions, now accept them as your own. When you keep everyone far removed from your heart to avoid getting hurt, you also hurt them, and hurt people hurt people."

Tears began to well in his eyes, but it was clear that years of conditioning kept them from falling completely. Then, weakly, he whispered, "I don't want to hurt people. I want to be loved. I want to be seen. The real me, in full."

"There's nothing stopping you from opening your heart. I can't promise that you'll never experience pain or heartache, but things can't continue as they are. You need to release your burdens. Let the people who love you love you."

"But I—"

"Baby steps. You don't need to jump into the unknown abyss right away, but you can start by listening more and opening up about how you feel. Don't be a passenger in your own life. Live it the way you want it to be lived. Live it to the fullest with others by your side and never let go."

"Thank you."

"I'll be right there by your side watching out from above. You'll be just fine. Just remember: You deserve to be loved, so allow others to love you."

When we returned to the Land of the Lost, Irshad seemed dumbstruck and completely lost for words. He finally spoke up. *I'm amazed. There was no empathic connection that entire time, and I know because I kept trying to get some sort of read on him. I don't really know how you managed to pull that one off. What made you think to speak the way you did?*

Flattered, I responded, "In short, it was just intuition. I think this man reminded me of my father. At first, I was irritated by his hateful provocations, but as I stepped back, I realized that the anger just came from a scared place. It wasn't so much that he was a spiteful person, but more that he was brainwashed into believing that the macho, tough guy act was the only way to be. Unfortunately, I think it's all too common for people to repress and keep others out of reach. Sometimes it can seem easier not to feel any emotion than to suffer heartache, but easier doesn't mean healthier. It's a generational problem where people forget to feel openly because they're afraid of coming off as weak or incapable. In some ways, I want to believe that my father is like this too. Maybe it's just because I want to humanize him, or maybe it's because I want to redeem him. I guess I'm hoping it's not an inability to love but merely a lack of understanding how to. Thinking like that makes even the worst of people seem a little more respectable. Using that same logic with this guy, it just became a matter of addressing the elephant in the room."

Well, my hat's off to you. Intuition or not, that was nothing shy of incredible. I may be an old man, but it would appear I haven't achieved infinite wisdom yet. Thank you for teaching me something.

11

The old woman and the young boy lay side-by-side. The distance between them consisted of two monitors and IV bags filled with what I suspected were chemicals for a cancer treatment session. There was just enough room between the equipment for one person to stand over them, one at a time, and review their progress. Medical professionals would step in and out often to check on them, occasionally replacing the bags and collecting data on the monitors. I had been watching over both of them since before this journey.

Prior to being diagnosed, the two were complete strangers. The elderly woman had been living a full life. Her youngest daughter had just brought a beautiful baby boy into the world. Her eldest son was on his way to becoming a senior associate at a start-up law firm that had been making big waves in recent years. The woman had lost her husband a while back, and while there were still plenty of older fish in the sea, she was satisfied with just her one love. She did, however, often miss him, and she talked to his portrait in the early mornings when she made herself tea and watched the sun rise in her backyard. Her children always found time to call, and she always found time to answer.

The young boy had just started middle school. He spent his afternoons playing with his buddies, pretending to be astronauts on some days and knights on others. No stick was too large to be a sword, and no land mass too unreachable to be a "new planet just discovered." He had a beautiful and loving family comprised of a younger sister — full of sunshine — and two loving parents to match that same energy. On weekends, the whole group would travel to their local reservoir and spend lunch by the water, eating homemade sandwiches and playing pirates.

After a full day of adventure, the group would go home and recount the excitement together while the boy's parents took care of chores and prepped dinner. Their nights would usually end with a movie together on a small couch made smaller by everyone pressed against one another.

While the two lived parallel lives that never intersected, they were connected by the presence of beautiful and loving families. In many ways, as I watched over them, I often found myself envious. I was certain each group had their share of troubles, but what I took special notice of was the bond they shared. No one had to feel alone or isolated. They all had each other, and there was nothing more glorious. Many a time when I would visit from beyond their realm, I imagined myself calling my loved ones just to talk or being smushed against a couch together as a single unit. I yearned for it.

One day, as the woman stared out beyond the horizon during a sunrise session with her late husband, she collapsed. It was sudden and nerve-racking, and I helplessly gazed on as she lay there in a daze. As per usual, her son called to do his daily ritual, but this time she didn't answer. Instead, three hours later — after panic had set in — he received a call from the hospital.

"Hello, is this Mr. Thompson? We're calling regarding your mother. We ask that you come down to the hospital center as soon as you possibly can… We have an idea of what happened, but we won't know anything until we run a few tests. Currently, she is stable, but the doctor thinks it's best if you and the rest of her family find your way down here."

The voice on the line was so cold. It was robotic and methodical. I wondered how many times that call had been made before to reach that monotone state. I asked myself, "How many times has that technician had to reach out to a family member knowing full well that the next journey that family embarks on will be arduous?" I was curious if that technician knew how many people made it through the battle, but maybe that's why the call felt so heartless. I imagine that after just a few of those calls, it would bear down on anyone.

Soon after Ms. Thompson's arrival, the young boy came in for a routine check-up. Outside of an abnormal cough and some mild pains, everything seemed normal, until it didn't. He too was admitted for further examination. The same voice that had spoken to the elderly woman's family now spoke to the child's.

"Hello, am I speaking with the parents of Charlie? We need him to come back to the medical center. There's been a development."

Suddenly, there were no daily calls or morning praises with late husbands. No morning teas or social hours. Now calls were signs of bad news, and no one wanted to answer the phone. What was once tea in a peaceful backyard was replaced by a hospital's chemical cocktail and bleak surroundings. Playing astronauts or knights was out of the question, too. Every discovery was a frightening concern and not just a new planet. Every stick was one that led to an injection, and the poor boy was no longer the one rescuing anyone, at least not from his bedside.

When it first happened, everyone remained hopeful. Instead of calls, the elderly woman received visits from her children whenever allowed. The boy couldn't play with his friends any longer, but they came in just to tell him that they'd come to rescue him. All he had to do was focus on getting better. Despite everything, both families remained as strong as they had been before. There was love and there was hope.

And soon enough, the little boy and the elderly woman were acquainted. Two parallel lives intersected. Two different stories collided together, impacting the lives of both families. Soon enough, two lives bonded eight together.

"Hi there. My name's Charlie. You remind me of my grandma. What's your name?"

The elderly woman felt weary despite finding the child's gesture sweet. She had a sad expression on her face, likely because she was also terribly saddened by the overarching reason why they were crossing paths in the first place. I'm sure she knew that she was getting older and believed that this sort of thing came with the territory of old age, but neither of them would have expected a child to be here as anything more than a guest. Finally, she said, "Well hello there, Charlie. I'm Janette. It's a pleasure to meet you."

Bursting with excitement, Charlie replied, "That's a pretty name. Hey, would you like to be my friend? I don't have any friends in here, and I don't want to be all by myself while my parents are away at work."

"I would love nothing more than to be a friend to you, little Charlie. I too could use a friend to be with in here. We're in this together now."

<u>12</u>

It was the start of something beautiful. Two strangers bonded together by a cruel reality only to remain hopeful, embracing the love given to one another. Charlie told his family all about Janette, who eventually got to meet them, and Janette was able to tell her family all about "little Charlie" who "added just enough spunk to keep things interesting around here."

Unfortunately, each day that passed scraped away at the hope that Charlie and Janette had, instead slowly building fear in their families' hearts. Time bore its full weight as both people became a little frailer with each passing session, and it was starting to create pressure on each family.

Janette's son was starting to fall behind on his work because of all the hospital visits. Her daughter was fighting two separate battles: managing the hospital bills and caring for her new baby boy. Soon enough, daily visits became weekly ones, which soon became bi-weekly. It was gut-wrenching to watch her family's strong hold begin to come undone at the seams. Even when her children did visit, they couldn't help but cry and panic. They were so scared of losing her that they began to distance themselves. I guessed that it was in the hope that if there was a fallout, they'd survive the initial blast. Another reason for their distance could have been that the sight of their mother withering was too great to bear. Despite all of this, Janette continued to present herself with a smile so that those around her didn't have to be afraid. Despite her position, she was still going to great lengths to protect her children. I knew Janette was accepting of her fate, but I also knew she was afraid. She would pray to her husband more frequently with each passing day, asking for more time to spend with their children.

"Oh, Harry. Our little babies are all sorts of worried about me, but they need to be worried about themselves! Besides, I know you're up there in the heavens watching over me, and little Charlie is still by my side fighting along with me. I won't pretend that I don't think about coming up there to see you, but in truth, I'm not quite ready. Please keep looking out for me and the little guy. We're doing our best to hold on."

Between Irshad's and my trips to other situations, I'd stop back in to check on the two. Sometimes one of them would just be asleep and the other would be talking with family. On longer respites, I would tune back in and listen to them speak with one another.

The little boy, curled up and shivering, began to speak. "Janette…"

"Yes, hun?" Janette said weakly by his side.

"I'm scared. I've been in here a long time now, and I don't think I'm getting any better."

"Don't be scared. It's all going to be okay. You just have to be strong a little longer, okay?"

"If I had been a good boy when I was healthy, maybe I wouldn't be like this. Do you think I deserve this?"

"Absolutely not, Charlie. You didn't do a single thing wrong. You've been good from the moment I met you, and I'm sure it didn't just start then. I'm sure you've been good all along. What makes you think you've done something wrong?"

"Well, Mommy and Daddy used to be full of love, but now all they do is shout and yell at one another. They seem so unhappy, and I think it's all because of me. We used to all play at the reservoir and watch movies and… and read bedtime stories, but now I don't think they do any of that. Mommy and Daddy are always busy now. My little sister cries more than ever now, and I think I've made our parents cry too."

His parents' misplaced anger and sadness weren't Charlie's fault; it was the condition he was in. I had been watching both families as Charlie's and Janette's conditions developed. Charlie's parents still had a lot of love for one another, but they were so afraid he wouldn't make it that it scared them. They helplessly watched as each chemo session took a small piece of him from them. They had watched a vibrant little boy become constrained to a world filled with cold rooms and harsh white lights. At home, they barely rested. When they put his little sister to bed, they'd stay up all hours of the night to review medical bills and discuss how to make ends meet. Unfortunately, the cost of getting better wasn't cheap, but they couldn't afford to stop his treatments either. I watched a constant battle of determining the best way to pay for his treatment. Whether it be to work extra hours and get advances on pay or consider getting a loan. They even considered begging and pleading for donations with anyone that would listen. The couch that his family used to pile onto together, the one that I had been so envious of, had been empty for so long now that the impressions on the cushions began to fade.

I found myself wondering how either family would afford the costs or what would happen when they no longer could. It reminded me of the first woman

I met with Irshad, and I imagined both families were feeling much like she had. I turned my attention back toward the group just in time to hear Janette's voice. "Listen to me, Charlie, your parents aren't upset with you at all. They're just scared because they worry about you. I get to see you almost every day, so I know just how strong you really are, but I think they miss out on that when they're looking in from the outside. All you need to do is keep giving them hope."

"Okay."

"Great. Now it's time for another round. Are you ready?"

"Yep!"

I continued to be amazed. I caught glimpses of their lives from far above, but that was all I could ever do. Each time I peered down to see them, I wanted to help. I wanted to be there rooting for them, but my presence would insinuate that something had gone awry.

Then one day, I was no longer peering from above. I was there, in the middle space between the two of them, amongst the machines. Janette and Charlie were right there on either side of me, connected to monitors and IV bags, withering away before my very eyes.

"No. No. No, no, no. Why am I here? Not these two. They have so much hope and love. I don't understand." And I really didn't. Why was I in this place with them? I looked up at their faces and saw the tears sliding down their cheeks, and that's when I realized why. Janette had been telling Charlie to stay strong and hopeful; she needed him to believe because she couldn't. Charlie wept because he wasn't sure how to be strong for her, for him, or for his family. With each passing moment that they didn't get better, the fear grew greater.

And as I stood before these two, I wept. Not because I had made an emotional connection, and not because my sorrow for them had overtaken my emotions. It was simply because I had grown to love these two strangers and didn't want to watch them die.

13

"Janette, Charlie. Can you both hear me?" I spoke softly. "Don't be alarmed. I'm just someone from above who's been watching over you both."

Too weak to speak, they both nodded.

"Amazing. Well, I'm here to remind you not to give up hope. You're both very strong, and I want you to push just a little further. Reach a little bit deeper and pull out all of the extra strength you can, okay?"

Another silent nod. Then Charlie finally spoke. "I'm scared. I'm not ready to go. I want to see my mom and dad and sister again. I don't want to die."

"I know, and I'm here to remind you that each passing day isn't something to fear. It's one day closer to seeing them again. Each step you take gets you one step closer to playing astronauts or knights with your friends, to movies with your family. Keep your hope because it can keep you alive. Both of you."

Finally, Janette reached out and ushered me closer to her side. When she looked up to see who was speaking to her, I watched tears well up and fall across her face. Through the constant, steady stream, she smiled and said, "Oh. You're just a child. It must have been hard on you to watch. I don't mean to impose, but may I ask you just one more favor?"

"Anything. Please let me help however I can."

"Just take my hand in yours and hold his hand too. Lend us that strength of yours we don't quite have anymore."

The old woman and the young boy lay side-by-side. The distance between them consisted of two monitors and IV bags filled with what I knew to be chemicals for a cancer treatment session. There was just enough room between the equipment for one person to stand over them, one at a time, and review their progress. Just enough space for one person to reach out their hands and embrace them both at the same time. Three souls connected together. There we were, holding on to one another in a cold and bleak room, desperately clinging to hope, asking for just one more day. There were no more words and no more exchanges. Just the loving embrace of three people in a tiny room meant for two.

Charlie was the first to close his eyes. The anxiety and fear had subsided, and he was finally able to rest. Janette held on for just a little longer. Before falling into a slumber, she spoke just once more, directly to me. "Poor baby. It must have been hard."

Back in the Land of the Lost, I continued watching the two.

Charlie woke up.

Janette didn't.

14

Soon enough, I was able to meet her once more. We greeted one another as friends this time, not as strangers. She explained that she knew she didn't have much time left in that world. Her "babies had already grown up. They'd be just fine," and she mentioned that her husband must have been waiting for her for quite some time.

"We don't usually contact the other side, but sometimes we make an exception for the recently departed. In this case, your husband asked that he be here for you when the time came. He should be right over there." As I pointed toward him, I watched these two kindred spirits reunite.

"So, you just couldn't stay away, could ya, my darling Janette?"

"You know me, Harry. Where you go, I'll always follow."

"Well, you certainly took your time getting here, huh?"

Janette laughed. "Of course. I had to make sure a few little babies were all safe and sound before I headed out. One little one, a boy named Charlie, especially needed a little extra loving. I'm hoping that by giving him the last of my strength, it was enough to keep him going."

"I know, my love. I've watched over you and our beautiful family every day that I've been away. My heaven couldn't really begin without you being here, but I was willing to wait as long as it took. Every day I watched you talk to me, and every day I answered back. Even when you got sick and your strength began to fade, I made sure to continue our conversation."

"You really are one of a kind, aren't you? The man I love with my whole heart and soul, and not even death could change that."

"Janette, the love we have is timeless and boundless, and even if it meant waiting ten more minutes, ten hours, ten days, or ten years, I still would have been here to accompany you to the afterlife. Heaven was missing an angel, after all. I'm sure they'll be ecstatic when they see I've brought her back with me."

"Oh, Harry. Before we go, let me just ask this little baby who watched over me in my final moments what will become of Charlie. I just need to know before I go."

I stepped in and told them both all about Charlie. After that night, he was finally in remission, and while it was still very recent and he was very weak, he never stopped talking about his good friend Janette. He talked on and on about how she was protecting him the entire time. She watched over him and held his hand through all the scary parts. The only reason, as he puts it, that he was able to pull through was her. His passing words to every curious ear were:

"I'll miss her. She was the best friend a boy could ever ask for. I hope I get to see her again one day. I'd like to thank her for keeping me safe."

And somewhere, in a realm just outside reality, three passersby waiting at a waystation stood watching over a little boy, unbeknownst to him. We all laughed and wept. We all knew this was goodbye, but even so, there was this odd sense of happiness around us. The type of happiness that brings you pain, but you understand and value its necessity all the same.

Before moving on with her husband, Janette embraced me and asked that when the day came for Charlie to pass, she'd like to be there to hold his hand once more, if she could. She asked that we all be there so the three of us could embrace one another one final time, just like we did the night she passed away.

And for the first time in a long, long time, I smiled.

"Absolutely. I look forward to seeing you both once more — a long, long time from now."

15

Still feeling the warmth of Janette's love, I began to wander back to Irshad, still light on my feet from the happiness I was able to take part in.

Daydreaming, I said to myself, "Days like this, as bittersweet as they are, make this job seem far more manageable. If all my visitors arrived after a long and full life, my existence would be far more rewarding. If we could all accept one another, faults and all, and show that same kind of love and compassion, what a beautiful world it would be. Certainly one worth fighting for. Definitely one worth living for."

Irshad appeared before me to serve as a reminder of this harsh new world. I was blissfully unaware and unencumbered, but that would soon change. My world was just moments away from thrusting anxiety upon me, and our impending conversation was at the nexus.

"Hey Irshad. What's with the cloudy aura? That's a little joke I've been working on seeing that we're bas—"

No time for pleasantries. We need to go. Now. It's happening, again. Just like last time.

I felt my chest tighten with each word. Panicking, I whispered to myself, "No. No. Not again. I'm not ready to fail again." I was afraid. I didn't want to lose anyone else the same way I lost that woman. Every single time I helped someone, I thought about her and all the ways I couldn't save her. It didn't matter how many times I had succeeded. It didn't matter how many souls were saved. To me, all that mattered was each soul I couldn't save. "How many heartbreaking moments must I endure? How many people must I watch crumble to lifelessness, asking themselves if there was ever any light to begin with and why it couldn't illuminate them, even for a moment?"

Irshad, who overheard me, responded, *As long as there are humans in this world and you remain here to help them, you will endure endlessly.* I could tell it wasn't meant to be a cold answer. It was the reply from a tortured man, burdened by eternity.

Just like before, we were thrust into a dimly lit world. This time, it was different. The second we appeared in reality, I recognized the setting. This was my town; this was my neighborhood, my house, my people. By the time I snapped back into the present, Irshad was sprinting in the opposite direction, shouting off from a distance to fan out and search the area. Both of us knew the stakes were too high to take our time, but I had a strange feeling that the person in need wouldn't be in this residential area. They'd likely be somewhere more removed and distant — a lonely place with a bridge and rushing water. A familiar place for me indeed.

I sprinted toward the edge of town, where the light was fading and the air tightening, all the while wondering if it was a friend of mine. Maybe they were dealing with the exact same thing I had been, and just like me, they didn't know where to look for help — or maybe they just felt like they didn't matter. Whatever the reason, all I knew was that getting there with time to remind them of their worth and value was most important, whoever it was.

As I continued toward my final resting place, it finally began to take shape. There was the lonely bridge, except now it had a memorial with a photo supported by the curb's edge and flowers just at the base of the frame. My photo. Beside the tribute created for me stood a figure, staring at the cold, rushing tide below. I remembered that feeling. Wondering. Contemplating. At the precipice between life and death, every second feels like an hour, and every hour feels like a second.

"Hey," I called out. "Hey there. Can you hear me? Why don't you take just a few steps away from that bridge for a little bit? Let's just talk for a moment, okay?" Suddenly the head shot up. I didn't know if I scared the figure, or maybe I was lucky enough to break a dangerous train of thought. "Hey. Seems like you can hear me after all. Well, I'd love to talk to you, if only for a moment. Is that—"

The figure turned to face me. First, I saw the hairs peeking through a hoodie — curly and chaotic. Then I saw tears, painted across a smooth face. Then came eyes, puffy and red, tired from all the pain. A pair of lips, bluish from the weather and quivering from the sadness, came next, and finally I saw the entirety of this person.

He finally spoke. "It's really you, isn't it? I thought I recognized your voice. You've been gone for quite some time now."

This lonely figure, shrouded in pain and searching for solutions in all the wrong places, wasn't just a familiar face. This boy, teetering on the edge between life and death, was my little brother.

16

Frozen in place, I couldn't speak. I couldn't even move. There was this deep, dark pit in my stomach, and my throat was starting to close. This panic was unlike anything I'd ever felt in either life or death. Before me was just a little boy, but his eyes had hollowed out and lost their glimmer. Whatever battle he was facing, he had lost repeatedly. Even though his heart was still beating, he was devoid of all warmth.

Finally, he spoke once more. "You heard me, didn't you? I said you've been gone a long time now. Where have you been? Huh? You know, when you decided to end your life, you ended mine too, but I had the misfortune to keep on living."

My heart sank. I was face to face with a direct consequence of my decision, and I didn't even have the courage to speak.

He continued, "Yeah, you heard me correctly. I'm sure you had no idea. How could you? You were already gone. The fact of the matter is you left me behind. My protector and my shield. You left me wide open to suffer."

Sheepishly, I coughed up, "Hold on. That's not fair. You had Mom and—"

"No. I'm not done yet. You lost your voice when you jumped, so do me a favor and use your ears instead. See, I idolized you. I wasn't blind to your pain and suffering. I knew just how bad Dad's treatment of us was, even at my age. Despite all of that, every day — even on your very last one — you always kept a smile on your face to shelter me. You always kept me warm with love and care, and you kept me safe. Did you know, the last day I ever saw you was when they lowered you into the ground? The first day of the rest of my life was my last day with you. It was the only time I saw you without a smile on your face.

Your protection ceased to exist, and I began to take a direct blast from Dad's wrath. Mom did her best, but even she was still picking up the pieces. Dad's solution to drown out his pain was to find solace at the bottom of every liquor bottle he could get his hands on. And it was in his drunken state that his rage was uncaged. Then there was me. I became an outcast in school. No one would approach me, and even when they tried, I was unreachable. There were days I just broke down regardless of the location or the time, and you know exactly how cruel kids can be. I became the new subject of their torture. They'd whisper things in my ears like 'Maybe it's your fault' and 'I would have killed myself too if I was related to you.' It was disturbing, but it constantly made me ask myself why you left us behind. What could I have done so wrong for you not to stick around? Why couldn't I save you like you saved me? Why did you leave me behind?"

"I, well, I—" I started to speak and then my voice gave out, and I was just mouthing the words. It wasn't that I couldn't say anything, and I certainly had things to say, but I just couldn't find the courage.

"Look at me. Look directly into my eyes and search for a shattered soul just trying to piece itself together. You'll only find remnants of it. I'm numb. And I'm tired. It's not like I don't have good days, and it's not like every day is some tragedy waiting to unfold, but I'm finding each day gets tougher and tougher, and the light of hope seems to get further and further out of my reach. At some point I started telling myself 'Fake it 'til you make it,' but somewhere along the way I forgot what part of me was real and what part I was faking."

And then he turned away, taking a step closer to the edge. One step closer to ending a story before it could finish.

There was another step.

And another.

Finally, I found some courage. At the line where life meets death — where I lost my own when I decided to jump — I mustered up the strength to say, "I'm sorry."

He stopped to turn back and look at me. "What did you say?"

"I'm sorry, and not just for leaving you behind and expecting you to pick up the pieces."

"Then what, exactly, are you sorry for?"

"I'm sorry that you've had to pretend for such a long time. And I'm sorry that you've had to fight for so long. I can see that you've played soldier so many times that I'm sure at one point you felt as though you weren't playing any longer. While I may never know the battles you've seen, I can see that each one has taken a piece of you. I know you feel hollow, and I'm sorry that you've had to cry alone. You are not the side character in your own story, and I really am so sorry that you've been made to feel that way."

"Just because you feel sorry for me doesn't change the way I feel. If all it took to fix people were kind words and warm sentiments, the world would never experience loss. We both know that's just not the kind of world we live in." He was at the very edge of the bridge now, leaning against the guardrails.

There were no more steps left to take besides the one that would send him over.

"Let me tell you something, not because I want to flatter you and not just because I want to help you, but because it's the truth, and you need to hear it. Loud and clear. If nothing else, listen to these words:

You are not some broken toy, cast aside and discarded, never to be loved again. You are not a burden, undeserving of care. You are not too far gone, ever, and most importantly you are not alone. Let me tell you what you are, though. You are loved. You are valued. Cherished. Every day you are alive is a blessing. You may question if the world is better off without you, and I will tell you — it is not. You mean something to someone. You are light, even when you feel surrounded by darkness."

As I spoke, I moved closer to him, right up until I stood in front of the scared little boy, face to face. I embraced him. His legs buckled under the weight of his sorrow, and together we sat on the safe side of the ledge, embracing and weeping.

"I know you're gone, but I really miss you. Not a day goes by that I don't."

"Not a day goes by that I don't wish I could take it all back. I wish I could have watched you grow up. Every day I wish I could tell everyone I knew just how much I loved them."

17

"So where do we go from here? Now that I'm at the bottom? I don't know where to start. I can't expect you to stay here beside me forever, can I?"

"I'm afraid not, but I can help you with what comes next."

"Oh? Well, what do I do now?"

"Live. Live, even when you feel like dying. Cry when you feel the need. Shout and scream when you must, but live on, and continue developing your story until it comes to its natural end. Seek help when you need it and remember to love yourself — even when it feels impossible."

"It's hard, you know? Living without you here."

"I'll always be here. I'm in your heart and in your memories. Try hard to remember the good ones of us."

"When will I get to see you again?"

"If I have my way, not for a long, long time. Live a beautiful life that even I get to enjoy as I watch from above. I'll always watch over you."

We hugged one last time, and then I disappeared back to my own realm with Irshad. Fortunately, it would be a long, long time until my little brother would see me again. Just as I had hoped for, he lived a long life filled with love and hope. A life I got to enjoy from the heavens.

Epilogue

Can I speak with you for a moment?

"Of course you can. Is everything okay? Do we have an emergency situation on our hands?"

No. It's not especially concerning, but it's more of a favor I wanted to ask of you.

"Whatever it is, I'd be happy to do it for you. In all this time together, you've never once asked me for a favor. It's the least I can do."

Thank you. Well, I do recall that at one point you had asked me how I even came to be here. 'Had I always been here?' or something like that.

"It's funny, isn't it? That almost feels like a lifetime ago. To think about how much has changed, how much I've changed since then. Look at how far we've come. All the people we've been able to help. It's beautiful, and I don't think I've ever properly thanked you for it, have I?"

It really is a night and day difference, isn't it? You've gone on to save countless souls, more than I could ever have imagined, especially given how new you are to this compared to me.

"Well, I'm flattered. But I think I should really be the one thanking you. So thank you, so much. You've been able to guide this 'lost one' to something greater than I could have ever imagined. Irshad, you are a gift. Now, please, what was that favor you wanted?"

Before that, I think I owe it to you to tell you a little bit about who I am, or rather, who I was. See, I actually wasn't the first guide. I had a teacher, just as I am your teacher. I didn't suddenly appear here one day. I was lost once. Long ago. I, just as you, couldn't find my way out of the darkness and I finished my story before it was meant to end. In so many ways, we share the same story, and we are of the same aura. Furthermore, Irshad isn't actually my name. It's a title, and I think you deserve to have that title.

"Oh, wow." I paused, letting his words sink in. "I always wondered, and I had some speculations as to your origin, but I never would've suspected all of that. I'm honored that you'd be willing to give me the same title as you, but I don't see that as much of a favor. Is there something you need me to do? Some final test?"

The only thing I ask is that you help me move on, to whatever comes next for me. Help me finally cross that threshold. Then, the title will be yours.

"Whoa. Whoa. Slow down. You realize what you're asking, right? You do realize how large that favor is, don't you? And moreover, how do you know that I'm capable of taking on this mantle of responsibility? I have, presumably, only a fraction of the experience you do. You've lived countless lifetimes."

That's exactly my point. I've lived countless lifetimes. I'm tired now. I haven't found rest since I originally passed away. I hadn't intended to ever retire until you came along. See, in all my lifetimes, I've never connected to souls in the same way you do. You've managed to pull off miracles that I couldn't have ever dreamed of, even when you were just starting. Saving your little brother, when he was just a young boy, all that time ago — that's when I knew you wouldn't just replace me, but you would succeed me. You are the true gift.

"I honestly don't know what to say. I can't imagine myself being ready for you to leave. I just don't know what I'll do without you there, guiding me on."

You'll do amazing. You don't need my guidance for that.

"Well, okay. I'm reluctant, but I would be honored to help you cross over. Bottom line, you deserve the rest. You may not have saved everyone, but you've done more than anyone else I've ever known. Not just for me, but for everyone you could reach. So, are you ready to get going?"

Thank you.

Suddenly, Irshad's older figure reverted to that of a young boy. The entity I only ever knew as old and wise shifted back to what he must've been when he had originally died.

Will you hold my hand until it's time for me to go? I'm scared.

"Of course I will."

Thank you.

"Oh. Before you do go, you mentioned that Irshad was a title. What exactly does that mean?"

He smiled. Then he said the last words I would ever hear from my teacher, my salvation, before he joined the countless souls he saved and tried saving alike.

It means The Guide.

Acknowledgements

This book may have been created from a single idea, but it was fostered by a wonderful support system that helped it blossom into what it is today. To that end, I'd like to acknowledge the amazing people that helped me create something so near and dear to my heart.

To my mother, you have my utmost gratitude. Not only were you at the forefront of my journey, always as an advocate for my success, but you also taught me to listen to people's hearts and dig beyond what is said. It is because of you that I strive to help others, both in person and in this book.

To my sister, you have my deepest respect. It is, in part, because of your journey that I was inspired to write this book. During your darkest moments, you confided in me that I was a source of light for you, and that has been the single greatest motivation for me to create something that aims to be a light for others.

To my closest friends, you have my highest admiration. Not only have you been a source of light for me in my times of need, but you've also opened up to me in your times of need. Your support with this book, as well as in life, motivates me to give my absolute best in all that I do.

To my talented cover artist, you have my greatest appreciation. Not only does your talent speak volumes for itself, but you have been amazing to work with. I find your passion for and devotion to creating a captivating cover to be extremely inspiring. Your insight and guidance have been an asset to this book's creation.

To my incredible editor, you have my highest praise. Your dedication and effort have been an incredible asset to me and to this book. Your opinions, both personal and professional, have given me great insight, and I look forward to any future collaborations we have.

To my dearest reader, you have my sincerest thanks. From the bottom of my heart, I would like to thank you for embarking on this journey with me. I hope that my book was able to reach your heart and remind you that you're never truly alone. Please continue to join me as I embark on future endeavors, and when the time comes that we meet, I look forward to listening to your story.

RESOURCES

While I hope this book finds a special place in your heart and on your shelf amongst others, I recognize that kind words may not be enough to help someone in need. If you found this book in a time of struggle, please allow me to offer a multitude of options that could be of some use to you. While this certainly isn't an all-encompassing list, and I can't take responsibility for the content, claims, representations, or the outcomes for any of these services, I do hope it helps you or a loved one. You have the power to save a life, even your own.

Hotline For Child Abuse Hotlines in the United States:

1-800-422-4453

1-800-222-4523 (hearing impaired)

Hotline For Missing or Exploited Children in the United States:

1-800-843-5678

Hotline for Crisis:

Text (USA): Text CONNECT to 741741

Text (Canada): Text HOME to 686868

Hotline for Depression:

1-630-482-9696

Hotlines for Domestic Violence in the United States:

1-800-799-7233

1-888-743-5754

1-888-215-5555 (California)

Hotline for Eating Disorders:

1-847-831-3438

Hotline for Elder Abuse:

1-877-353-3780

Hotline for Parents and Families in a Crisis Situation:

1-800-840-6537

Hotlines for Rape/Sexual Assault:

1-800-656-HOPE

1-877-995-5247 for members of the DoD (Department of Defense)

1-212-227-3000

1-866-966-9013 for legal support in every state. This also provides referrals.

0845-303-0900 (London Victim Support)

514-934-4504 (Montreal, Quebec)

613-562-2333 (Ottawa, Ontario)

416-597-1171 (Toronto, Ontario)

0808-802-9999 (United Kingdom National Helpline)

250-383-3232 (Victoria, British Columbia Women's Sexual Assault Center)

Hotline for Self-Injury:

1-800-366-8288

Hotlines for Substance Abuse and Alcoholism:

1-800-234-0246 (Alcohol Abuse and Crisis Intervention)

1-800-234-0420 (Alcohol and Drug Abuse Helpline and Treatment)

1-800-390-4056 (Alcohol and Drug Addiction Resource Center)

1-800-331-2900 (Support and Information)

Suicide Hotlines in the United States:

1-800-784-2433

1-800-273-8255 (Prevention Lifeline)

1-800-799-4889 (Prevention Lifeline in Spanish)

Text: 1-800-799-4889

Hotline for International Suicide:

519-416-486-2242 (Ontario)

1-888-787-2880 (Alberta)

1-866-872-0113 (British Columbia)

514-723-4000 (Quebec)

852-2382-0000 (China)

592-600-7896 (Guyana)

1566-2525 (South Korea)

495-625-3101 (Russia)

0861-435-787 (South Africa)

0800-181-0721 (Germany)

92-22-307-3451 (India)

44-0-8457-90-90-90 (Ireland)

3-5286-9090 (Japan)

143 (Switzerland)

08457-90-90-90 (United Kingdom)

Hotlines Youth/Teen Crisis Intervention:

1-800-448-3000

1-866-488-7386 (LGBTQIA+ Youth)

Text: "Trevor" to 1-202-304-1200 (LGBTQIA+)

Text: TEEN to 839863 (Teen text line)

1-877-968-8454 (Youthline)

1-800-448-4663 (International Youth Development Crisis Hotline)

Suicide and Crisis Lifeline

988 (Text or Call)

www.ingramcontent.com/pod-product-compliance
Lightning Source LLC
Chambersburg PA
CBHW010801310726
48974CB00006B/935